Gods of my Fathers

Kyuka Lilymjok

i

ISBN 978-978-954-756-2

Published by:
Free Pen Publishers
10 Lachlan Close Maitama, Abuja

Any people depicted in stock imagery provided by Thinkstock are models, and such images are being used for such purposes only.

This book is printed on acid-free paper.

Because of the dynamic nature of the internet, any web address or link contained in this book may have changed since publication and may no longer be valid. The views expressed in this work are solely those of the author and do not necessarily reflect the views of the publisher, and the publisher hereby disclaims any responsibility for them.

To the god of freethinkers

A counterfeit
Is always less than the
shadow of the
original

Passage One

Well, my father warned me before his death. But I didn't heed his warning. This is the result. I am haunted by the Gods of my fathers. I don't even think it is only a case of being haunted. I think it is one of being hunted.

Now my father was a tall imposing man of forbidding presence. Those who knew him said he was not only a masquerade but an oracle in his own right. Some people went as far as saying he was an incarnation of one of the Gods of the land. My father in his bearing towards people and circumstances affected the air and manners of what people said he was. He had a regal walk and spoke in a piercing booming voice. His gaze was fixed and concentrated and his smile was fleeting and was as meaningful as what he said. All these qualities of his accentuated in him the presence of the deity people said they saw in him. Whenever he stood to talk in the assembly of elders of our village, people not only listened, some people trembled.

When I was a young man growing up, I once overheard two elders of our village talking about my father. 'I have always believed Agenle is one of the Gods of our land,' I heard one of the elders saying. 'Look at the way he walks and talks; look at what he says and the way he says it.'

'You are right Ame,' the other elder said. 'Look at even the colour of his eyes and the hang of his nose. Look at how his lips are set whenever he is not talking. A god surely lives in that man.'

'Not only do people tremble whenever he is speaking, the earth sometimes also trembles whenever he is speaking,' Ame said. 'I believe when he walks a path or enters a river, the path or the river shivers.'

'It is a family thing,' the other elder said. 'His father was like that though I do not see this thing in his son. His son looks to me like the tail of a dog on a lion.'

'You have said something here Nkuchi,' Ame said. 'Dendo looks to me like the fawning one that would rubbish the greatness of that family.'

Hearing the two elders talking so highly of my father and so lowly of me really made me sad and mad at them. Swallowing my anger, I walked away without them knowing I overheard them.

As a child, I used to accompany my father to his little shrine in the woods. It was by a big bongo tree near a little stream. On the lower portion of the stem of the bongo tree were red and white markings. By the markings were masks and figurines that represented my ancestors, the Gods of my fathers; my Gods as my father said.

'If they are my ancestors, how can they also be my Gods?' I asked my father one day when we were at the shrine.

'Taah!' my father screamed. In this scream and the way he stood, his eyes fixed on me, I could see and feel the presence of a God in him. 'Your ancestors are also your Gods,' I heard him saying in a matter-of-fact voice after his anger had subsided to a tranquil level. 'As it has been with me, it would be with you. Your ancestors are also the Gods of your fathers, your Gods.'

Not wanting to annoy him further, I didn't say anything more.

There was a little clearing at the foot of the tree where his shrine was. The clearing was hedged by thistles planted by my father. Inside the clearing were little fine stones in three rows. The fine stones were spirits of the forest that attended to the Gods of my fathers.

Twice every week, we worshipped the Gods of my fathers in the shrine. We sprinkled libation on the masks and figurines on the stem of the tree and poured it on the rows of fine stones in the clearing. All the while my father would be performing these rituals, he would be telling the ancestors, our Gods, to secure us from evil and give us only what we need for sustenance.

What I did with my father, my father said he did with his own father and expected me to do with my son. If I fail to do so, our ancestors, our Gods will feel neglected and will haunt me till I die. I did not take my father's words serious and so did not adhere to them. Shortly after his death, I abandoned our ancestors as I saw his Gods and became a Christian.

For years nothing happened. Well, I did not expect anything to happen. That nothing happened firmed up my attitude to my father's bidding. Suddenly, things began to happen; things I couldn't trace to the Gods of my fathers until much later.

I was living with my wife and children in Bonte. One night while we were asleep, the roof of my house began to shake violently as if there was a violent wind outside. I was terrified the roof may be blown off. Well, it was not rainy season, so I did not fear my property would be soaked by rain. But that it was not rainy season was reason for me to be terrified. Violent winds that blow off roofs do not blow in the dry season. I opened the main door to my house to see conditions outside and was surprised to find them calm. There was no storm or any noticeable wind. No house beside mine was experiencing what my house was. This fact alarmed me far more than the violent rocking of the roof. For a while I hung by the main door not knowing what to do.

As abruptly as the rocking of the roof started, it stopped. I was relieved it stopped, but was also terrified it stopped. The evil forebodings I had for its happening, I had for its stopping.

For days, I pondered over what could be the meaning of the strange happening in my house that night. Where I come from, this was not the sort of thing you resolve by pondering. It was the sort of thing you go to a marabout for divination. But my Christian faith would not allow me go to a fetish diviner. The pastor it would allow me go to for spiritual intervention, I also did not go to until another strange occurrence befell me.

Passage Two

I liked walking the woods, particularly the woods of my village. Walking the woods of my village, I found the peace I could not find in the village itself. Whenever I was in my village, I went into the woods before going to anyone's house. Even at night, particularly moonlit nights, I used to go to the forest. Walking the woods, I was always full of cheer and peace.

One evening I was in my village, I went out for a walk in the woods as usual. Deep in the woods, someone called me so close at my heels that I thought if I turn, I will brush my face against his. However, when I turned, there was no one. My heart leapt down in fear. It can't be. While I was still in shock and fear, a hairy hand brushed against my face. I passed out.

When I came to, it was dusk. I ran back home sweating in the worse fear and panic I had ever known. At home, I could not immediately relate my experience to anyone. I was too frightened for that. It was the following day I was able to tell my mother. That night I could not sleep. The experience kept coming at me like a revolving nightmare. I was back in the woods several times with the hairy hand brushing against my face the several times I was back there.

When I told my mother my experience the following day, her first reaction was disbelief. When she looked at me however and saw the look of fear and sheer panic in my eyes, she began to credit my frightful tale with belief.

'You had such a horrendous encounter and kept it to yourself all night?' my mother wondered more to herself than to me. 'Your behavior is as strange as the tale you just narrated to me.'

'When I returned home yesterday, I was too shocked and frightened to talk,' I said. 'It is only this morning I find my voice.'

'I have always warned you to stop going into the forest,' she said in a heavy tone. 'The forest is full of evil spirits.'

'But people go into the forest all the time.'

'Yes, village people go into the forest all the time. Evil spirits of the forest are not excited by village people; but they are by city people like you. They are excited by city people the way bees are excited by perfume which in a way you are.'

'It was so terrible.'

'We will have to see Abuyi over this. He will divine what happened and offer a remedy.'

'I am a Christian and can't go to Abuyi, a fetish priest.'

'If your Christian God were so strong, he shouldn't have allowed what happened to happen.'

'Neither could Abuyi.'

'Abuyi could not because you are not his follower. My child, use your head and not that of the white man. Abuyi was here before your new faith came. You were visited yesterday by a spirit. Abuyi knows this spirit because it is a local spirit. Since he knows the spirit, he would tell it to leave you alone.'

'I will not go to Abuyi,' I said, thick headedly.

'Neither will I sit by watching you refuse to go to him,' my mother said in an authoritarian tone that brooked no dissent from me. Such was the authority in her voice that I could not say anything again. My silence told her I had acquiesced in her proposal. She also did not say anything again.

Throughout the day, I watched her making preparations for our trip to Abuyi the following day. In the evening, I snuck out of our house with my bag and returned to Bonte where I narrated my experience to my pastor. Like my mother, his initial reaction was one of disbelief. When he got to believe me, he said the devil is a liar. For a brief moment, sinfully I wondered who the devil was lying to. He prayed for me and told me it was well with me. Though I knew it was sick with me, I believed him and went about my affairs sure I was free from further strange experiences.

Passage Three

After three weeks at Bonte, I was again walking the woods in the forest between Bonte and Twangwa. When I could not walk the woods of my village because I had not travelled to the village, I walked this forest. Most weekends I spent in Bonte, I went to this forest to walk the woods. After walking for a long time this day, I lay down under a tree to rest, and sleep swept over me. While sleeping, I found myself in a land I knew people I had never seen or met before. The earth was blue and people walked in little clouds. Everyone I saw was completely encased in a cloud. This included me, for as soon as I arrived the land, I was encased in a cloud. Though I was in a cloud and they were in clouds, I could clearly see their faces. As I stood staring at this strange land in awe, I saw my father moving towards me. Behind him were my other forbears to the hundredth generation. They were all in tears. At that time, I did not know what they were crying about. It was much later I found out the reason for their tears.

Apart from my father, all my other forbears were dead when I was born. So, I did not know them. However, in this land I knew everyone without the benefit of introduction. I stood looking at my father slowly moving towards me carrying along with him the long line of my ancestors that looked like a long train in slow motion. When my father got to me, he leaned his head towards mine. As he did so, all my other ancestors leaned their heads towards each other's. As soon as this was done, the clouds we were in lifted us into the air in spiral arc. We flew through the air in the spiral arc formation for a long time before landing on a cloud in the sky. It was then my father spoke for the first time.

'Dendo, look down here and tell us what you see,' my father commanded me.

I looked down and saw Jewish worshippers in a Wailing Hall. I realized we were perched on a cloud over Israel.

'What are they doing there?' asked my father.

'They are worshipping God,' I answered.

'Which God are they worshipping?'

'The God I worship."

'The God you worship comes from somewhere; where does he come from?'

'He comes from Israel.'

'Excellent. Gods like people are natives. They don't belong everywhere. They belong to places, not space. The God you worship is a Jewish God.'

'Abomination! Blasphemy! The God I worship is everyone's God!' I screamed.

'Taah!' my father screamed.

I was back to his little shrine in my village where he once screamed at me this way. I was back to where I was eavesdropping on Ame and Nkuchi talking reverently about my father.

'Be careful you don't abominate or blaspheme your own Gods in your zeal for an alien god,' I heard my father saying in a hard, grating voice. 'You are before your own Gods.'

'I am sorry, please, forgive me,' I said, subdued by his voice.

'Good,' said my father in a soothing voice that in fact soothed me.

Around us, spirits moved to and forth exhaling forcefully. I later came to know they were exhaling the stench of my not sticking with the Gods of my fathers. Now and then the sky retched like one about to vomit. I also later got to know the sky was retching from nausea provoked by my not sticking with the Gods of my fathers.

Passage Four

After a while of saying nothing, my father began to talk again: 'Know that the God you worship is not your own God, but the God of the Jews. His name is even Jewish. His name is Yahweh.'

'This is tough on me,' I murmured. Though it was only a murmur, my father heard it.

'We know,' he said. 'It is tough for a dog to accept it is a stupid thing.'

'This is crushing me,' I murmured.

'We know. The truth has a crushing edge.'

'There is only one God.'

'Cut out that crap; only dogs bark that way.'

'I am sorry.'

'Sorry for what you said or thinking there is only one God?'

'For what I said.'

'Then you are not sorry; you have not repented of your folly. Saying there is only one God is not half as foolish as thinking there is only one God.'

'Why?'

'Because thinking there is only one God forms the basis of the foolish belief there is only one God.'

'I see,' I said without quite understanding what he said. Not quite understanding what he said, I was not seeing what I said I was seeing.

'There are as many Gods as there are races, tribes and clans,' I heard him saying. 'In fact, there are as many Gods as there are human beings.'

'Why are there as many Gods as clans, tribes, races and human beings?' I asked.

'Good question, our child. There is God and there are Gods. There is the One in Many God. It is this God that expresses himself as the genius of a race, a tribe, a clan or an individual. Expressing himself this way, he is the God of races, tribes, clans and individuals – the Many in One God.

'Hmm …,' I hummed.

'Genius is a God. Every race has genius. It is the genius of a race that created it and defines it. As it is with race, it is with tribe, clan and individuals. Every tribe, clan and individual has genius. It is the genius of a tribe, clan and individual that created and defines the tribe, clan and individual.'

'Hmm …, I hummed again.

'The Bible does not lie when it says there are three Gods: God the Father – the One God in Many Gods; God the Son – the racial, tribal and clannish Gods who are the Many Gods in One

God; and God the Holy Spirit – the personal Gods who are also Many Gods in One God. The racial Gods enjoy their own trinity: There is the mystical African God, the imaginative and creative Jewish God, and the thinking Asian God. The mystical African God wishes to manifest himself in the attitude of Africans but is thwarted by the dog mentality of Africans that made them abandon their Gods for other people's Gods. The imaginative and creative Jewish God manifest himself in the attitude of Jews who abide with him. The thinking Asian God manifest himself in the attitude of Asians who abide with him. Our attitudes are the manifestations of the Gods in us.'

'What!'

'Yes. God the Father – the One in Many God, has a purpose expressing himself the different ways he does through the races, tribes, clans and individuals. Those who worship their own Gods help the One in Many God achieve his purpose; he is happy with them and blesses them. They excel in life. Those who worship the Gods of others instead of their own Gods frustrate the purpose of the One in Many God. He is not happy with them and withholds greatness from them.'

'My ancestors ...'

'That is how it is our child. Beyond the racial, tribal and clannish Gods, there are the personal Gods. The many in one God expresses himself in the individual as in the race, tribe and clan as genius. Genius expresses itself in the individual as talent. The talent of a man is a God in him. It is that God your bible says will feed a man. It is that God that made a man a God. It is that God the Igbos call *Chi* – personal God.

'Everyone has talent. The only reason a person is born is to realize his talent. If he is not able to realize his talent at the time of his death, he is reincarnated to realize it. Once he realizes his talent, he is free of reincarnation and ascend into the spiritual realm as a spirit – a God.

'Hmm ...'

'It is not only languages the One in Many God desires to be different and many, he desires Gods to even be more different and many. To achieve this, he manifests himself as different Gods in all the races, tribes, clans and individuals of the world.'

'My ancestors ...'

'There is God and there are Gods. We, for example, are Gods – the Gods of your fathers who were humans before but had realized our talents; ascended the spiritual realm and are now custodians of the genius of the clan through who the One in Many God expresses himself.'

'Hmm ...'

Passage Five

As I was humming, we again flew through the air and landed on a cloud.

'Dendo, look down here and tell us what you see,' my father commanded me.

I looked down and saw Japanese Shinto worshippers in a shrine. I realized we were perched on a cloud over Japan.

'What are they doing there?' asked my father.

'They are worshipping God,' I answered.

'Not a God, but Gods.'

'Gods?'

'Yes, Gods.'

'Which Gods?'

'Shinto Gods.'

'Shinto Gods?'

'Yes, Shinto Gods.'

'Shinto Gods. I have never heard anything like that.'

'I bet you haven't. You are in the belly of the Christian faith and don't know Jack from Tom.'

'Shinto Gods; who is Shinto?'

'Maybe what is Shinto is a better question.'

'What is Shinto?'

'Shinto is the way of the Gods.'

'Which Gods?'

'Japanese Gods.'

'Japanese don't have Gods separate from the God of other people.'

'Taah! Have you forgotten what we said about every clan, tribe and race having their God?'

I shrank from the whip of this scream. This scream that expressed the vehemence and resentment of my father for things that did not help the worship of my ancestors will never lose its terror to me.

'Japanese have their own Gods as any race has,' I heard my father saying while I was yet to regain my composure. 'Shintoism is all about Japanese Gods.'

'What is Shintoism?' I asked.

'Shintoism is the way of the Gods. But it is not only the way of the Gods; it is the way of Japanese people. The way of Japanese people is shaped by the Asian thinking God that makes Japanese to learn and imbibe what is good from other people. The One in Many God expresses himself as the Japanese God that settles the Japanese genius of learning and imbibing what is good in the culture of others.'

'Hmm…'

'The Japanese God creates the Japanese genius that makes Japanese so intelligent and inventive.'

'Yes, what makes Japanese so productive?'

'The Japanese God.'

'The Japanese God?'

'Yes, the Japanese God. The One in Many God expresses himself not only as the Japanese genius but as the Japanese intellectual tree.'

'Japanese intellectual tree?'

'Yes, Japanese intellectual tree that taps knowledge from other races.'

'What is this intellectual tree like?'

'It is like every fruit bearing tree you know.'

'Like a mango or orange tree?

'Yes, like any of these trees.'

'Please, explain to me what the Japanese intellectual tree is all about.'

'The Japanese intellectual tree taps knowledge from other cultures. Like every other tree, this tree has roots, stem, branches, leaves and produces fruits according to season. Genes and genius are the roots of the tree. Genes and genius produce consciousness which is the stem of the tree. Consciousness produces culture which is the big branches of the tree. Culture produces language, religion, art and science which are the small branches of the tree. The small branches produce the virtues of religion and the products of science and art – the leaves of the tree.'

'This sounds logical.

'It is logical. The Japanese genius that believes in tapping intelligence from other races is a genius that believes in many ways to earthly as heavenly salvation. Believing in many ways to earthly as heavenly salvation, Japanese genius taps not only from its own ways, but from the ways of other races. Its own ways and the ways of other races are the ways of the Japanese Gods which Shintoism is all about. In the Japanese genius, no one is dogmatically imposed as the only way to heavenly salvation. The One in Many God expresses himself as the Japanese God that allow free thinking. By free thinking, Japanese accept and reject Gods, create and reject science and technology. By the Japanese genius, there is always another way to think and get things done, not only one way of thinking and getting things done.'

'Hmm...'

Passage Six

Again, we flew through the air and landed on a cloud.

'Dendo, look down here and tell us what you see,' my father commanded me.

I looked down and saw Hindu and Buddhist worshippers in Hindu and Buddhist shrines. I realized we were perched on a cloud over India.

'What are they doing there?' asked my father.

'They are worshipping God,' I answered.

'Which God are they worshipping?'

'I don't know; but may be Indian Gods.'

'Good, we are happy you are coming round. These are Indian Hindus and Buddhists worshipping Indian Gods – the Many in One Indian Gods.'

'Which Gods are the Many in One Indian Gods?'

'Purusha for instance, is a Many in One Indian God that Hindus worship. In Buddhism founded by the Buddha, every Buddhist is a God. So, there are as many Gods in One God in Buddhism as there are Buddhists.'

'Every Buddhist a God?' I asked in shock. 'I thought since Buddhism was founded by the Buddha, he is the God of his religion.'

'Your thinking is logical, but the Buddha is not a God, at least not a God for Buddhists,' said my father. 'According to the Buddha, everyone is a God through who the One in Many God expresses himself. So, if the Buddha is a God, he is a God only for himself, not a God for Buddhists.'

'Everyone a God?'

'Yes, everyone is a God says the Buddha. No, not says the Buddha, but says the One in Many God that expresses himself as the Buddha. Thinking being what makes a person a God, thinking is the God in the person. Thinking being the God, every Buddhist has to save himself by thinking which leads to nirvana or enlightenment. It was this character of Buddhism that excited Chinese into embracing Buddhism though it was founded by an Indian.'

'Thinking a God; so shocking!'

'Not so shocking bearing in mind that thinking is a genius thing, bearing in mind that thinking is what makes a person – his fortune or misfortune. The One in Many God expressing himself as the Indian God and Indian genius hoists thinking over Indians.'

'So very exciting.'

'Great! 'The One in Many God manifest himself in India as the Many in One God through Hinduism and Buddhism. He manifests himself as a Many in One God of thought. If Indians are intelligent, they are intelligent because thinking inspired by their Gods is cultural with them.'

'Hmm ...'

'Thinking is what inspired the four noble truths of the Buddha.'

'The four noble truths?'

'Yes, the four noble truths.'

'What are the four noble truths of the Buddha?'

'The four noble truths are: all life is suffering; the cause of suffering is desire; a cessation of desire is a cessation of suffering; there are eight ways to end desire, to end suffering and attain the salvation of enlightenment.'

'This is very, very interesting. What are the eight ways desire might be ended?'

'According to the Buddha, desire might be ended by right views, that is, a true understanding of the four noble truths. Right intent; that is, a true desire to free oneself from attachment, ignorance and hatefulness. Right speech; that is, not lying, gossiping or engaging in hurtful talk. Right conduct; that is, abstaining from hurtful behavior as killing, stealing and careless sex. Right livelihood; that is, making your living in such a way as to avoid dishonesty and hurting others including animals. Right effort; that is, preventing bad habits from arising again while good qualities should be nurtured. Right mindfulness; that is, focusing of one's attention on one's body, feelings, thoughts and consciousness in such a way as to overcome cravings, hatred and ignorance. Right concentration; that is, meditating in such a way as to realize imperfection, impermanence and non-separateness.

'This sounds really good.'

'Yes, it does, but don't become a Buddhist because Buddhism is for Indians and you are not an Indian.'

'Chinese are Buddhists.'

'Yes; but they are also Confucians. If a good percentage of Chinese are Buddhists, it is because Confucianism as Buddhism is founded on thought, on the Many in One Asian God of thinking.'

'Who are Confucians?'

'Confucians are those who worship Confucius a Chinese sage.'

'A sage being made a God?'

'Yes. When Buddhism was making serious inroad into China, Chinese authorities to protect the Chinese genius proclaimed Confucius a God.'

'What!'

'Yes, that was what happened. However, perhaps what the Chinese forgot when making Confucius a God was that Confucius was a thinker like the Buddha and making him a God was a case of old wine in new bottles. It was the case of an Indian God wearing Chinese clothes. Because Confucianism is Buddhism in essence, Buddhism still prevails in China. Yeah, the Many in One God expresses himself as the Asian God of thinking. In China, he expresses himself through Confucianism; in India through Buddhism.'

'The Buddhist worshippers are motionless. Why are they so motionless?' I asked taking my father back to the Buddhist worshippers.

'They are motionless in body, but in mind very active. They are meditating, thinking. They are worshiping the Many in One God of thinking by thinking.'

'Worshiping the Many in One God of thinking by thinking?'

'*Yes,* worshiping the Many in One God of thinking by thinking. Indians are brilliant not necessarily because their genes possess higher intelligence quotient, but because they are moved by the Many in One Asian God of thinking to think more than others.'

'Great!'

'Yes, great, not only for Indians, but for the world. When a race, tribe, clan or person harnesses its or his genius by sticking with its or his Gods that express its or his genius, not only it or him benefits, but the whole world benefits. Similarly, when a race, tribe, clan or person fails to harnesses its or his genius by abandoning his Gods that express its or his genius, not only it or him suffers, the whole world suffers.

Passage Seven

'The One in Many Gods expressing himself as the Jewish God of imagination and creativity propels Jews to imagination and creativity,' I heard my father saying.

'Hmm ...'

'To keep others outside intelligence and allow Jews to imagine and create, the Jewish God of imagination and creativity inspires Jews in Judaism to chant.'

'Does chanting inspires imagination and creativity?'

'It sure does.'

'How?'

'Chanting is a stable emotion that opens up the eyes of the mind to see what is in the world of imagination and creativity.'

'Hmm...'

'The One in Many God expressing himself as Yahweh – the Jewish God of imagination and creativity who expresses himself as a jealous God. He jealously wants the Jews to be the ones exclusively imagining and creating things just as the African mystical God wants Africans to be the ones exclusively in charge of mystical things.'

'So touching and heady.'

'Yes, so touching. To keep Jews imagining and creating things, Yahweh – the Jewish God of imagination and creativity keeps Jews from Christianity, from singing and clapping.'

'What!'

'Yes.'

'Why should singing and clapping prevent Jews from imagination and creativity?'

'How can you imagine or create anything when singing and clapping? Singing and clapping are riotous emotions that shut the eyes of the mind from seeing things in the world of imagination and creativity.'

'Hmm ....'

'Can you see the point?'

'Yes, I can. But if singing and clapping in Christianity is against intelligence, how come Christians are intelligent?'

'Halleluiah Christians, praise the lord Christians, singing and clapping Christians are not intelligent. It is sober and reflective Christians, that are intelligent.'

'Hmm ...'

'The Jewish God so much wants Jews to imagine and create that he even inspires them to unbelief if this will lead them to imagination and creativity. He is prepared to annihilate himself for the   Jews   to   prosper.'

'What!'

'Yes. Realizing fears of offending God can interfere with imagination and creativity, the Jewish God of imagination and creativity now and then incites exceptionally intelligent Jews to disbelief in him.'

'Hmm ...'

'Doing so well by imagination and creativity, the Jews imagined their God created the world and the entire universe. They imagined their God would be the one that would end the world, condemning sinners and rewarding righteous men.'

'What!'

'Yes. Yahweh the Jewish God committed to advancing the Jews, annihilates himself in the minds of imaginative and creative Jews so that they can imagine and create freely.'

'Hmm ...'

'From Karl Marx to Albert Einstein to countless other distinguished Jewish scholars, atheism and free thinking made them who they are.'

'Hmm ...!'

'This is how it is. Even Moses and Jesus celebrated for their faith may not be believers for all you may not know.'

'Abomination.'

'Be wary of abominating your Gods.'

'What!'

'This is how it is. The Jews moved by an imaginative and creative God deny the existence of God and have since been looking out for themselves, and in a way their God, in atheism.'

'Incredible!'

'Unfortunately, it is true.'

'My ancestors!'

'That's how it is.'

'Yahweh not only excites Jews to unbelief, he also excites their agnatic Europeans to unbelief for the sake of imagination and creativity.'

'Agnatic Europeans?'

'Yes, agnatic Europeans.'

'Are Europeans agnates of the Jews?'

'Yes, they are.'

'How?'

'The Jews are a wandering people. The wandering Jew is a progeny of a wandering race. In the course of their wandering in Europe, the Jews intermarried with Europeans resulting in Europeans becoming Jews in genius.'

'What!'

'This is how it is.'

'But Americans are also intelligent.'

'Who are Americans? Americans are Europeans that migrated to America after the Jewish genius has absorbed the European genius.'

'Interesting!' I exclaimed.

'That's how it is our child,' said my father in a declarative tone. 'Americans and Europeans are not different from Jews,' my father went on in a very assertive voice. 'Americans and Europeans are Jews and Jews are Americans and Europeans. Jews have so fused into Americans and Europeans that the two have become one.'

'This is something!'

'Yes, it is something.'

'Can this be the reason Jews control the world?'

'It is partly the reason. But the main reason they control the world is that Jews led by their imaginative and creative God possess the best form of intelligence, and intelligence as you know controls the world. There is no promised land flowing with milk and honey different from the Jewish head. When the Jews fled Egypt, they did not flee it to any promised land flowing with milk and honey, but with the promised land on their necks. Canaan was a barren land they were to offload or pour the milk and honey in their heads on to make it fruitful.'

'My ancestors...'

'With milk in their coco, with their promised land flowing with milk and honey in their heads, with a legendary imaginative and creative genius, the Jews control the world in different ways.'

'Hmm ...'

Passage Eight

'What of the Arabs?' I asked with bated breath after a while of thoughtful silence.

'Those ones; they are not different from Africans. Islam is an imitation of Judaism. The Arab genius is inside the belly of the Jewish genius. The One in Many God expresses himself as Allah – the God of poetry and wealth among the Arabs. However, instead of the Arabs worshipping Allah with reference to Arab ancestry, they worship him with reference to Jewish ancestry. To be free of Jewish domination, Arabs must lean their religion away from Judaism. For Arabs to be the equals of Jews, Allah the Many in One God for Arabs should be the equal of Yahweh and not an imitation of Yahweh. Arabs domination by Jews is a Godly and genius thing. To be free of this domination, Arabs must regain their own genius founded by their God.'

'This is really, really serious.'

'Yes, it is because it is true.'

'It appears what you are telling me about Jewish domination of the world is true. But why do the British also dominate the world?'

'Like I said, Europeans are Jews and Jews are Europeans. Britons are Europeans; so, they are

Jews. That apart, the world uses English language; so, the owner of the language should control the world. It is not for nothing that serious nations insist on using their own language. They know the imperial and intellectual implications of doing otherwise. Even to think, you need a language. The person whose language you use to think controls your thoughts. If he controls your thoughts, he controls your action. If he controls your action, he controls you. Nations that insist on using their own language have reduced the influence the British have on them. Remember, language is one of the small branches produced by the genius tree.'

'I remember,' I said in awe of all my father had said. 'If I may ask, what are Buddhists meditating about?' I asked taking my ancestors back to Buddhism which has so much excited me.

'About life, how to attain the four noble truths.'

'This sounds great.'

'Yes, it does. But like we said earlier, don't become a Buddhist. Buddhism is for Indians.'

'I can see your point,' I said in a cheerless tone.

'The Jews, the Japanese and the Indians have kept their genius because they are true to their Many in One God,' I heard my father saying. 'We have all seen the result of doing so in the intellectual prowess and resourcefulness of the Jews, Japanese and Indians.

'We can indeed all see,' I enthused.

'Yet, imagine a world birds and animals are flying planes and driving cars and trucks which if they have intelligence, would have been inspired or incensed by the Jews and Asians creative and thinking genius to produce.

For a moment, I was horrified by the spectre of what I was asked to imagine; by the noise and sight pollution of it.

'While Jews, Europeans, Americans and Asians have realized their genius, Africans and Arabs have not,' I heard my father saying. 'Africans have abandoned their Many in One God, have allowed themselves to be taken over by alien religions and languages and we all see the result of doing so.'

'Things are really bad for Africa,' I mourned.

'Yes, they are. You are so poor you can't even afford your own God or language. From lacking a God and language, you came to lack a head. All these because you abandoned the African genius. All the negativisms Africans exhibit are fallouts of Africans not being themselves,

abandoning their genius settled by their Many in
One God.'

Passage Nine

'What is the African genius settled by African Many in One God?' I asked alive with enthusiasm.

'The African genius is mystical,' said my father with uncommon zeal. 'It is a genius settled by the African mystical Many in One God. But it is mystical in a positive way.'

'Mystical?'

'Yes, mystical. It is the African genius generated by the African mystical Many in One God that has been flying you in the clouds from country to country since you arrived here,' said my father.

'I don't understand.'

'What don't you understand?'

'How the African genius could have been flying us about?'

'But you understand we have been flying about?'

'Of course, I do.'

'If you do, we are saying it is the African mystical genius generated by the mystical African Many in One God that has been flying us about. The African genius as we said earlier is mystical;

but mystical in a positive way, not the negative way it has been twisted to manifest itself.'

'I also do not quite understand what you are saying here.'

'We never expected you to understand so easily matters of this depth. The mystical African Many in One God is more spiritual and sensual than intellectual. So the African genius he generates is more spiritual and sensual than intellectual.

'Mystically speaking, genius from its Roman mythology conceptualization is the guardian spirit of a place or person. This mystical Roman genius is a kindred spirit to the positive African mystical genius. Again, under Roman mythology, genius is seen as a demon or supernatural being. This type of genius is what the African genius has been twisted to be instead of genius that is a guardian spirit.'

'Who twisted the African genius into a demon?' I asked in a woeful tone.

'Africans themselves.'

'Too bad,' I said in a plaintive tone

'Yes, too bad,' said my father. 'Finding two types of mystical genius, Africans instead of going for the positive went for the negative genius that manifests itself in witchcraft and human sacrifices.'

'Why did they make such a choice?'

'There are three reasons. The first reason is what you know: What is bad carries a seductive aroma. Africans were seduced by the seductive aroma of negative mystical genius. The second reason is that the choice of a negative mystical genius happened at a time men's mental faculties had not developed to appreciate how to harness the positive mystical genius to advance themselves. All people were thinking of at this time was how to deal with people they imagined were out to harm them. Thirdly, slavery and colonialism also did not help the evolution of a positive African mystical genius. Caught in the web of slavery and colonialism, all Africans thought of was how to use mystical powers to do harm to their enslavers and colonial masters. If you can remember, in South Africa, there was a point some African Leaders thought of using African Juju to chase away the Apartheid regime.'

'What you are saying might be true. But why have Africans not switched from the negative to the positive mystical genius in today's world; now that primordial fears of harm, slavery, colonialism and apartheid are gone?'

'Bad habits die hard. In the course of bad habits dying hard, the African negative mystical genius has tragically become the African genius. Again, Africans that could have helped the evolution of a positive African mystical genius are either Christians or Moslems. This has further thwarted the evolution of a positive mystical genius.'

'You mean Christianity and Islam are in the way of the evolution of a positive African mystical genius?'

'Without doubt. Christianity and Islam are frustrating the evolution of a positive African mystical genius. If all Africans were worshiping the mystical African Many in One God instead of the Jewish Yahweh or Arabs Allah, these Gods would have generated in them the positive mystical genius thus freeing them from the negative mystical genius.'

'The positive mystical genius you are talking about, what would it have accomplished for Africans?'

'It would have led to Africans flying without the need for aircraft.'

'You mean that?'

'Yes, I mean that. Like I said earlier, it is the African mystical genius that has been flying you in the clouds from country to country since you arrived here.'

'Incredible!'

'Yet, it is true. It is the African mystical genius positively evolved that flies us about here in clouds. Japanese, Americans and Europeans lacking this genius cannot fly here; they trek.'

'You are not by any means joking?'

'We have no one to laugh to jokes, so we don't joke here.'

'My ancestors!'

'An evolved African mystical genius would have made planes and all other automobiles unnecessary; so it would have spared horses, donkeys, camels and other beasts of burden the ordeal of carrying humans around.'

'My ancestors!'

'That is how it would have been. Africans have failed and disappointed the One God in Many who expressed himself in Africa as a mystical being and genius complementing the genius of the Imaginative and creative Jewish God and the genius of the thinking Asian God. The One in Many Gods wants, Jews to imagine and create things, Asians to think things out and Africans to fly things about.'

My ancestors!'

'That's how it is our child.'

'If Africans have failed to develop the positive mystical African genius, how do we come by the positive mystical genius that has being flying us about?'

'A very good question our child. We came by the positive mystical genius that has being flying us about by our great ancestors who worshipped the Many in One mystical African God. The Many in One African Mystical God grateful for his worship by our great ancestors settled the positive mystical genius that has been flying us about.'

'If the worship of the Many in One mystical African God by our great ancestors can generate the positive mystical genius flying us about, we need not worry. When we die and arrive here, we will benefit from what our great ancestors did.'

'Witless child. It is not only flying here we are talking about. We are talking about Africans flying the living about now, not only flying the dead here. A developed positive African mystical genius would have been moving living people and goods about instead of planes and other automobiles thus saving the world the financial, time and environmental cost of moving people and things by automobiles, thus sparing the world the crude mechanics of modern technology. Moving people and things by mystical means would have also saved the world loss of lives and properties occasioned by automobile crashes. As they say, imagine a world without automobiles on the ground and planes in the air. Imagine one without all the noise, dust, smoke, light and sight pollution.

'I was thrilled to my bones by the world I was asked to imagine.

Yes, the development of the positive African mystical genius would have spared the world the crudities of science and technology!' I heard my father saying.

'My ancestors,' I murmured.

'The development of a positive mystical genius would have led to people eating frees in the air, being shielded from the sun by clouds, from the rain by rain shadows and from cold by *tespit*.'

'My ancestors!'

''That is how things would have been, my child.'

'What are frees?'

'Frees are like the manna the Israelites fed on in their journey through the desert to Canaan. It is a meal supply from the universal substance just as manna.'

'How would people have been shielded from the sun by clouds?'

'By the magical power of *giwan*. The magical power of *giwan* when well-developed makes clouds walk or fly over men wherever they are going.'

'My ancestors! How would people have been shielded from rain by rain shadows?'

'By the same power of *giwan*. By the power of *giwan*, rain dries up as it nears where people are sleeping, sitting or standing.'

'My ancestors!'

'That's how it is our child.'

'How would tespit have shielded people from cold?'

'Tespit is a shawl or a duvet in the universal substance. It keeps you as warm as the womb keeps an unborn child. To put it plainly, tespit is a womb in the universal substance.'

'My ancestors!'

'That's how it would have been our child.'

What is this universal substance you keep referring to?' I mumbled in awe of all my father had said.

'It is what you walk through but cannot see; it is the air you breathe in and out!'

'My ancestors!'

'Not only has the refusal of your generation to worship the African mystical Many in One God prevented the evolution of a positive mystical genius to move people and things around the world, to feed, clothe and house humanity, it would also stop flying by mystical means in the hereafter if you do not return to your Gods.'

'Why should our refusal to worship our Gods stop flying by mystical means in the hereafter?'

'Because the positive mystical genius our great ancestors evolved flying us about here is about wearing out. Unless by your worship of the Many in One African mystical God you generate another positive mystical genius to replace the expiring genius, we will in the nearest future be unable to fly the way we are now. That is why we are angry with you for abandoning for alien Gods the Many in One African mystical God that fosters the positive mystical genius. A positive mystical genius is the nimbus cloud that flies us about in the hereafter. We are crying because with unworthy offspring that run after other races Gods instead of their own, we will soon be without clouds to fly us about.'

'This is something.'

'More than something, this is serious.'

Passage Ten

For some time, there was silence. I was thinking about the so many things my father had said to me and it seemed he was giving me time to do so.

'As you have explained to me the Japanese intellectual tree, explain to me the African intellectual tree,' I said after a while of deep thought.

'The African intellectual tree?' asked my father.

'Yes, the African intellectual tree or don't we have any?'

'You do have an intellectual tree; only it does not bear positive fruits.'

'Why does it not bear positive fruits?'

'Because you abandoned your Many in One God, Africans instead of evolving a positive mystical genius, developed a negative mystical genius,' my father said, bitterly.

'This is sad.'

'Yes, it is sad,' said my father in a melancholic voice. 'The African genius either bears negative fruits or no fruits at all.'

'Bear no fruits at all?'

'Yes, bears no fruits at all. Because its fruits bearing genes have been inhibited or sterilized by foreign religions and foreign languages, the African genius bears no fruits. As you have already seen, one God expresses himself through different Gods. The different Gods generate different geniuses for the different races, tribes, clans and individuals they are Gods to. Races, tribes, clans and individuals can only excel by expressing the genius generated by their Gods. Africans having no God of their own instead of expressing genius express folly.'

'My ancestors ...'

Africans worshiping alien Gods have tried expressing genius outside their own Gods, but it is all in vain. You can't cut off the small branches of a mango tree, then engraft those of a tenge tree and expect the tree to still produce mangoes. Alien religions and alien Gods are branches of the tenge tree engrafted on the African mango tree and therefore it can't produce mangoes.'

'It is very clear to me now,' I said in a voice that assured my father it was clear to me.

'We are happy to hear you saying this. We will be happier seeing you acting what you said you understand.'

As I stood still in wonder of all my father had said, I could see a lot of wolves milling about us. 'Why all these wolves?' I asked my father.

'The wolf is a genius,' my father said. 'Because geniuses are Gods and the wolf is a genius, we respect wolves a lot here. That's why we have so many wolves about us. You haven't seen a dog here, have you?'

'No.'

'A dog is the opposite of a wolf. A dog is not a genius but an idiotic thing. Taming took away all the feral character of a dog where genius resides leaving a teddy thing. The wolf howls; there is genius in a howl. The dog barks; there is imbecility in a bark. The dog is an African. The wolf is an Indian, a Japanese and a Jew.

'Hmm ...' I hummed.

Passage Eleven

'Listen to the baying and growling of the wolves,' my father said.

I listened and could hear a low, steady humming sound that soon translated into the baying and growling of the wolves. From baying and growling, the wolves about us began to howl in a long haunting stream that made the hair on my head to rise.

'What is this all about?' I asked my father in a broken voice.

'It is time to go for a wolves'funeral dance in the moon.'

'A wolves' funeral dance in the moon? What is it about?'

'When we get there, you will know.'

'Where is the moon?' I asked. I asked because I could not see any moon. Though there had been no moon or stars, there had been no darkness either. On the contrary, there had been a brilliance by which things could be seen beyond mere form to identity. The source of that brilliance I could not tell. At some point, I thought the clouds we were wrapped in and the wolves about us were the sources of the light, but I could see no light either in the wolves or the clouds.

'Soon you will see the moon,' my father said.

As soon as he said this, a moon and stars appeared above us. With the coming of the moon and stars, the place became much brighter and clearer. As I stood wondering about these sudden appearances, the wolves rose into the air and sped towards the moon in a long spiral pound. They were closely followed by my ancestors and me. For the flight to the moon, my father took hold of my hand as his own father took hold of his hand and all my other ancestors took hold of each other's hands and we flew towards the moon. Later, my father told me that this was how the wolves' funeral dance in the moon was always attended. The wolves always led the way followed by the ancestors. Being a wolves' dance, the wolves should lead the way to the dance.

We landed on the moon in no time. All about the moon was dark. But where we were was lighted by a huge campfire. All wolves and the ancestors were illuminated by the fire. This fire is different from any fire I have ever seen. It is pure white, as white as snow. Because of the nature of the fire, it created an island of day in a sea of darkness. Again, there were no faggots fueling the fire. The fire sprung from the bare moon without any trace of faggot. Yet, the fire cracked and cackled as if fed by faggots.

Passage Twelve

When we landed, the funeral dance was yet to commence. But wolves were everywhere by the fire wagging tails, swaying heads and occasionally howling into the night. It was a weird spectacle to behold. A giant wolf was by the fire, so close to the fire that I wondered why it was not scorched by the fire. I later learnt this wolf was the chief of the wolves and fire does not burn the chief.

The chief was furrier than the other wolves and looked more fierce and rude. His feral aspects were not tampered by any gaiety about him, but were rather accentuated by a woeful atmosphere that roamed about him.

'Is the funeral dance for a wolf that has just died?' I asked my father.

'Yes,' my father replied. 'Death and life mingle so much among wolves.'

'Even among humans, life and death mingle.'

'Yes, they do; but more so among wolves.'

'How?'

'Whenever a wolf dies, two wolves are born immediately to replace the dead wolf.'

'I see,' I said in astonishment.

'A wolf's genius lies in a pack. A wolf achieves its best only in a pack,' my father said in a. concentrated voice. 'It is for this reason that procreation is very important to wolves. It is for this reason wolves refuse to be domesticated. The wolves' funeral dance in the moon is to mourn the death of a wolf and to celebrate the birth of two wolves to be born to replace the dead one.'

'A wolf's genius lies in the pack, what does that mean?'

'It means a wolf excels only in a pack. Without the pack, a wolf cannot be anything; it cannot excel. It cannot even survive.'

'Why?'

'Because that's the genius of the wolf. Alone, a wolf is a coward. But in a group, a wolf is a symbol of courage. In a pack, a wolf can attack the elephant knowing the pack is there to assist it. Without the pack, a wolf is wary of attacking an antelope. A wolf is only a limb of his clan. A wolf cannot live outside community. In fact, the life of a wolf is not in it but in its community. Community is to the wolf what the shell is to the tortoise. Without the shell, the tortoise is dead.'

'Wonderful!'

'Yes, wonderful.'

'A wolves' funeral dance,' I murmurred, my mind going back to the wolves' funeral dance.

'Yes, a wolves' funeral dance,' my father intoned in a deep voice. 'Whenever you see a wolf howling at the moon at night, it is howling at a wolves' funeral dance in the moon it could not attend.'

'What!'

'That's how it is.'

As soon as my father stopped talking, the wolves began the funeral dance. It was the weirdest thing I had ever seen. It was spritely, springy and in a queer way, graceful and stately. Wolves leapt into the air and howled into the fire in a thunderous and spine-tingling fashion.

My ancestors soon joined the dance. It started with my ancestor farthest from me. Of all my ancestors, the one farthest from me was the tallest. He was so tall that were I to stand near him, my height may not go beyond his waist. In addition to being tall, he wore a long beard and had a bald head and a horse face that was soft and friendly in its bearing. He leapt into the air like a Masai dancer, then began a slow but deliberate walk-dance of the ancestors. He was followed by the ancestor next to him until the dancing came to me.

We danced into the wolves as they danced into us. The surface of the moon which before the dance was stony was now a little supple. The air which before the dance was dry was now a little damp and moist. The fire which before the dance was snow white had gone ashen, turning us into ghostly shadows and phantoms. While the wolves danced and howled, we danced and sang. Howling wolves asked life to tell them its meaning. Life answered that it has only one meaning: that every living thing should be the best it is capable of being. In singing, the ancestors asked life what a man will do to be the best he can be. Life answered that a man must tap into his genius to be the best he can be.

Passage Thirteen

The dance went on for a long time before it stopped. When it stopped, the fire again turned snow white and the island of day again returned to the part of the moon we were. The head of the ancestors spoke. A hush fell on wolves as on us when he began talking. Man has genes. Wolves have genes. The genes of man produce his genius. The genes of a wolf produce his genius. The genes of a man and the genes of a wolf are settled by the Gods of men and the Gods of wolves who men and wolves must worship for their geniuses to express themselves excellently.

'Genius generated by the Gods of a man's or a wolf's ancestry produces the best man and the best wolf. A wolves' funeral dance on the moon mourns the death of a wolf and celebrates the birth of two wolves. But it also celebrates the purity and fruits of genius produced by the Gods of wolves' ancestry.

Unlike the wolves here, our progenies have breached and betrayed our genius. They mooned around the world without purpose and without excelling in anything except folly. We have brought one of them to this funeral dance in the moon to be mooned,' he said in a voice reeking contempt. 'Dendo, step out to be mooned.'

I stepped out in shock and awe.

Wolves and my ancestors all aimed their bare buttocks at me. I was mooned for abandoning the Many in One African mystical God and by extension my genius to become a dog. This was the ultimate act of denunciation and scorn.

My heart lurched and I woke up with a start. It was dark. Night had since fallen. It seemed I had slept for a long time. In deep thoughts, I began walking towards where I parked my car. The more I thought over what I went through while sleeping in the forest, the more I was convinced it was not a dream, but a revelation. If it was a revelation, Gods of my fathers, what can I do? How do I uproot an alien God with deep roots in the lives of your descendants and plant you in his stead?